BOTS

THE MOST ANNOYING ROBOTS IN THE UNIVERSE

by Russ Bolts
illustrated by Jay Cooper

LITTLE SIMON
New York London Toronto Sydney New Delhi

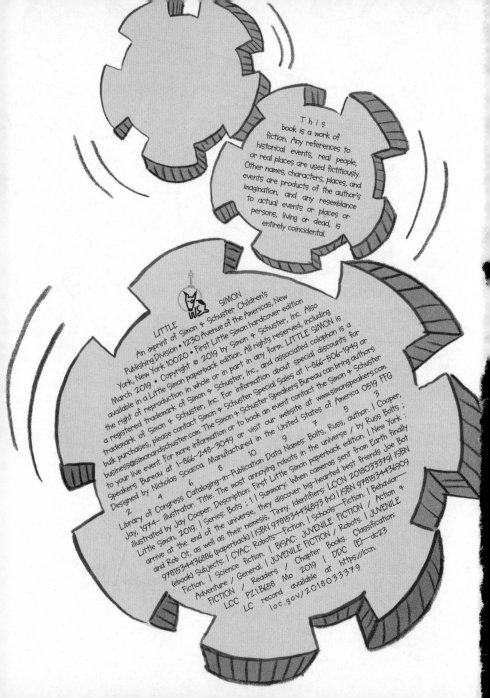

LITTLE SIMON
An imprint of Simon & Schuster Children's Publishing Division • 1230 Avenue of the Americas, New York, New York 10020 • First Little Simon hardcover edition March 2019 • Copyright © 2019 by Simon & Schuster, Inc. Also available in a Little Simon paperback edition. All rights reserved, including the right of reproduction in whole or in part in any form. LITTLE SIMON is a registered trademark of Simon & Schuster, Inc., and associated colophon is a trademark of Simon & Schuster, Inc. For information about special discounts for bulk purchases, please contact Simon & Schuster Special Sales at 1-866-506-1949 or business@simonandschuster.com. The Simon & Schuster Speakers Bureau can bring authors to your live event. For more information or to book an event contact the Simon & Schuster Speakers Bureau at 1-866-248-3049 or visit our website at www.simonspeakers.com. Designed by Nicholas Sciacca. Manufactured in the United States of America 0519 FFG

2   4   6   8   10   9   7   5   3

Library of Congress Cataloging-in-Publication Data Names: Bolts, Russ, author. | Cooper, Jay, 1974- illustrator. Title: The most annoying robots in the universe / by Russ Bolts ; illustrated by Jay Cooper. Description: First Little Simon paperback edition. | New York : Little Simon, 2019. | Series: Bots ; 1 | Summary: When cameras sent from Earth finally arrive at the end of the universe, they discover big-hearted best friends Joe Bot and Rob Ot, as well as their nemesis, Tinny. Identifiers: LCCN 2018033379| ISBN 9781534436893 (hc) | ISBN 9781534436886 (paperback) | ISBN 9781534436909 (ebook) Subjects: | CYAC: Robots—Fiction. | Schools—Fiction. | Behavior—Fiction. | Science fiction. | JUVENILE FICTION / Robots. | JUVENILE FICTION / General. | JUVENILE FICTION / Action & Adventure / General. | BISAC: JUVENILE FICTION / Action & Adventure / General. | Readers / Chapter Books. Classification: LCC PZ7.1.B658 Mo 2019 | DDC [E]—dc23 LC record available at https://lccn. loc.gov/2018033379

CONTENTS

CHAPTER 1

Deep Space

Many years ago, scientists on planet Earth created a space camera. They wanted to see what was at the end of the universe.

 1

It was the perfect size to put in a rocket ship. These rockets would carry the cameras across the universe to discover whatever was hiding in deep space.

Plans were made. The rockets were built. Soon, all of Earth watched as the scientists started their countdown.

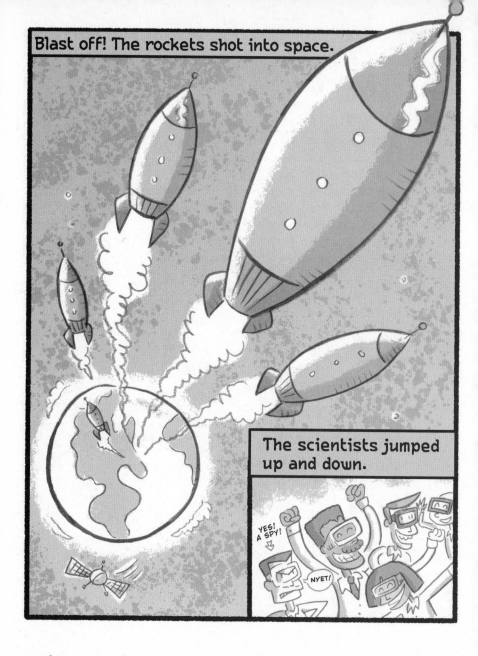

6

The rest of the world waited . . .

And waited . . .

And waited . . .

And waited, because the universe is a really big place. The rockets made their way through the stars, past the planets, and into the great beyond.

9

The people on Earth went on with their lives. Most of them even forgot about the rocket ships and the space cameras. They were too busy doing things on Earth to worry about outer space.

As years passed, even the scientists lost track of the rockets. They thought the space cameras were lost forever.

Maybe they fell into a black hole?

Maybe they crashed into a comet?

Maybe they were captured by aliens?

No, wait, that's silly. There's no such thing as aliens.

Then one day, everything changed.

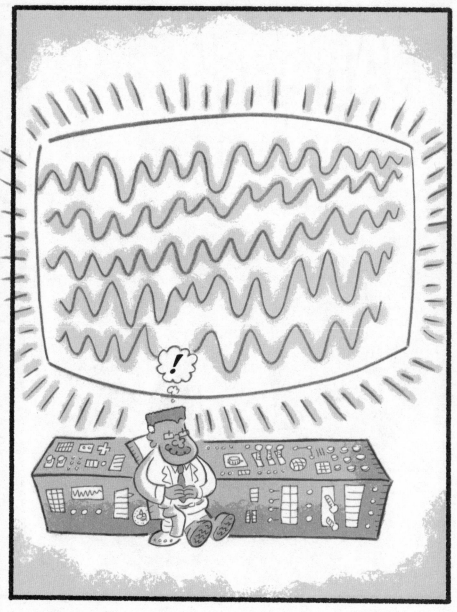

The space cameras began beaming back the first pictures ever from the end of the universe. It appeared to be . . . an alien planet.

The planet was made of metal, like a planet-size spaceship.

There was a very big sign on the planet that read: Mecha Base One.

The rocket ships were not alone. There were other spaceships zooming around the planet too. That could only mean one thing:
ALIENS LIVED AT THE END OF THE UNIVERSE!

The other spaceships did not seem to notice the Earth rocket ships at all. Just like people on Earth, the aliens on Mecha Base One went on with their lives.

BLOOP!

Hhee!

The Earth rocket ships were made to stop at the end of the universe, so they landed on the planet.

Then the rockets released all the space cameras.

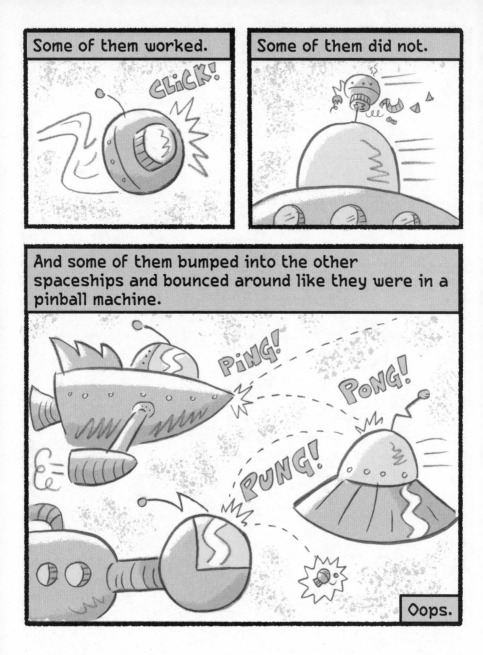

The space cameras that made it through unharmed showed a planet that was very futuristic. "Futuristic" is another way to say that these aliens must be very, very, very, very smart.

Then the space cameras found two aliens!

Earth was finally going to meet the very first creatures from outer space . . .

. . . but nothing prepared them for this.

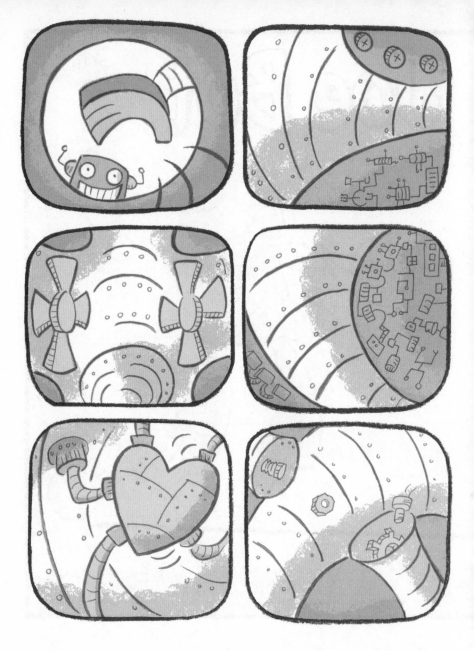

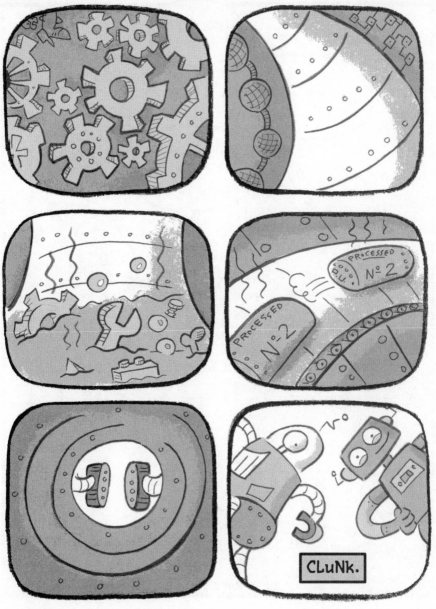

27

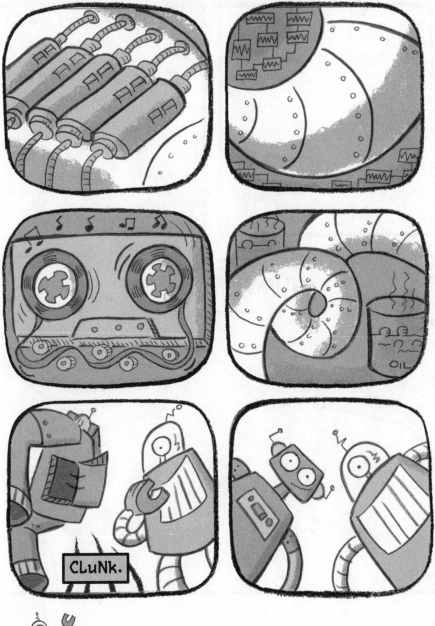

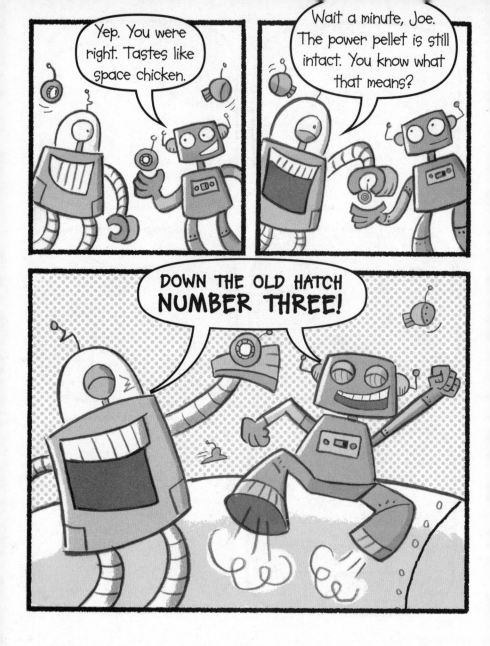

Well, that was unexpected. Hmm, maybe the space cameras had not found the smartest life-forms on this planet. Still, it was fun to watch.

33

CHAPTER 4 Dude, It's a Camera

It would be nice to say that Joe and Rob only ate the space camera three times. But they took turns eating the camera . . .

all . . .

35

36

38

And so the robots tried to figure out what in their world this strange object could be.

44

There is a great deal of evidence to support this fact.

Before long, every kid on planet Earth was watching the Bots. Even some of the children's pets started watching the show too!

This is how one scientist also stumbled onto the Bots.

But I am not important to this story.
Let's get back to the Bots.

ENGLAND

INDIA

KENYA

SOUTH KOREA

56

You see, when children love something, other children start to love it too.

Pretty soon Joe and Rob were on every screen in the entire world.

BRAZIL

JAPAN

HAWAII

EGYPT

But maybe that was what made Bots so fun to watch?

CHAPTER 6

Botsburg

Back on Mecha Base One, Joe held the floating camera.

Then he saw even more cameras floating around them. Cameras that had been filming them the entire time.

So Joe and Rob reset the cameras to follow them everywhere around their hometown of Botsburg.

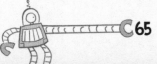
C65

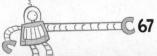

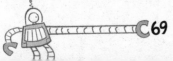

Back at Rob's house, his parental units did not seem to mind the cameras. In fact, they did not notice them at all. Rob had a very big and very busy family.

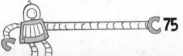

Do not worry. The book is not broken.

Half of the cameras stayed at Rob's house.

The other half of the cameras followed Joe home. What happened next was very exciting.

Earth was about to witness its first Bot nighttime routine.

Dinner.

Reading time.

89

CHAPTER 8

Good Morning!

ZzZzzZzzZzzZz

E-Z FLOAT SLEEPER 3000

Wow, that was amazing. But now, it's boring. Hmm, perhaps we should fast-forward.

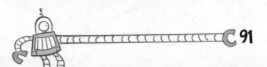

After getting ready, Joe and Rob met at the school bus stop. Lots of other Bots were waiting there too. That didn't stop Joe and Rob from doing their secret-best-Bot-friend handshake.

Handshake

Pretzel

Gimme Five

Rump Bump

Wow, that was amazing. But now, it's boring.
Hmm, perhaps we should fast-forward.

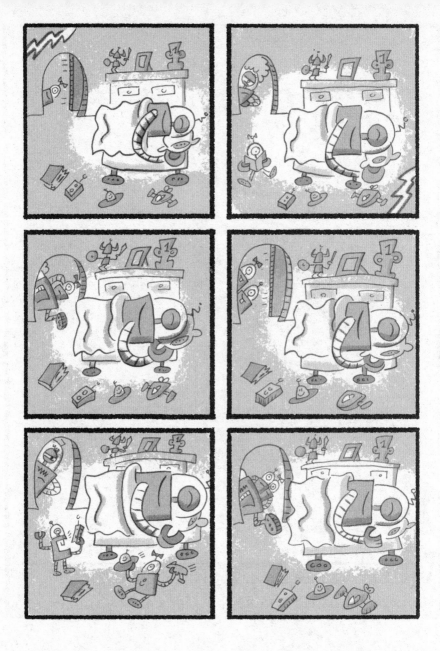

As Joe and Rob waited for the school bus, none of the other Bots paid attention to the cameras. Perhaps they thought the cameras were new students?

Well, almost none of the other students paid attention to the cameras.

Fellow Earthlings, I have a bad feeling about this Tinny Bot.

Luckily the bus came just in time. Actually, it didn't look like a bus. It was moving way too fast.

It wasn't a bird.

It wasn't a plane.

It was a rocket! A school bus rocket!

CHAPTER 9

Bot School

The school day on Mecha Base One started just like a school day on Earth.

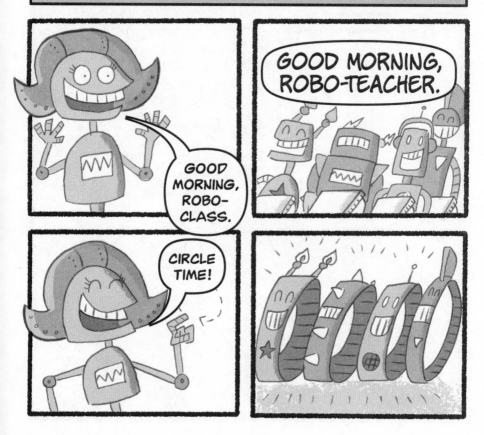

108

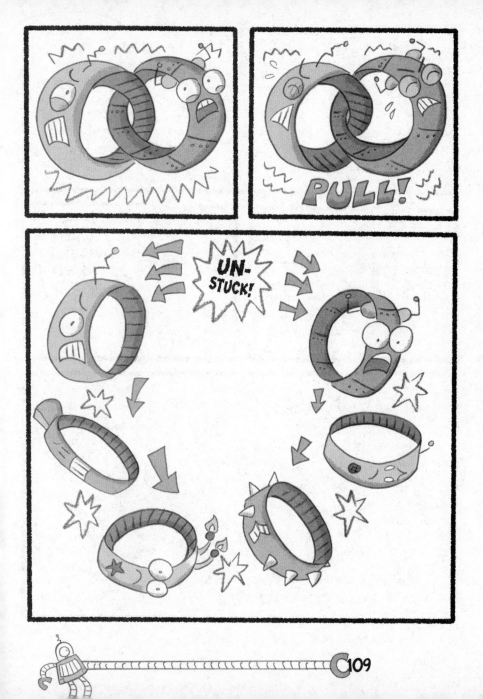

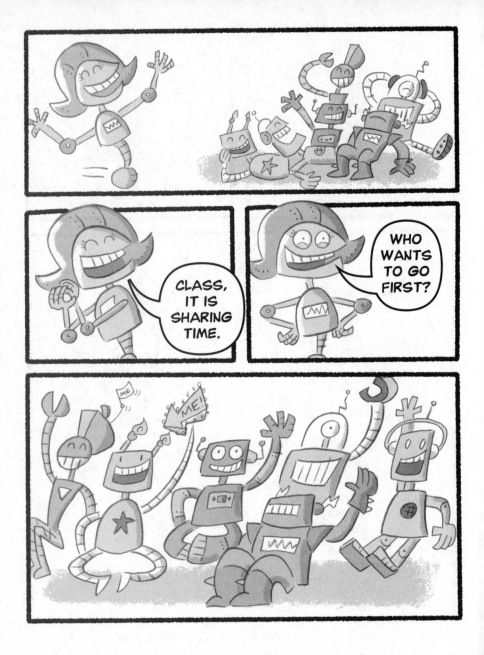

CHAPTER 10

The Mystery Tower

The rest of Bot School was fun, but not very exciting until the end of the day. Let's fast-forward.

After school, Joe and Rob went to their favorite place in all of Mecha Base One. The playground.

Ha! Ha! Ha! Ha!

At last, I have you, camera. And at last
I have you, whoever is watching this camera.
My name is Tinny Bot, but you can call me
SUPREME RULER OF ALL!

TUNE IN NEXT TIME FOR...

#2

BOTS

THE GOOD, THE BAD, AND THE COWBOTS

by Russ Bolts illustrated by Jay Cooper